The illustrations in this book were painted in gouache and colored pencils on sabretooth paper.

Heidi

Copyright © 1996 by Loretta Krupinski

Library of Congress Cataloging-in-Publication Data
Spyri, Johanna, 1827–1901.
    Heidi / Johanna Spyri ; retold and illustrated by Loretta Krupinski.
        p.   cm.
    Summary: A Swiss orphan is heartbroken when she must leave her beloved grandfather and their happy
home in the mountains to care for an invalid girl in the city.
    ISBN 0-06-023438-5. — ISBN 0-06-023439-3 (lib. bdg.)
    [1. Grandfathers—Fiction.   2. Mountain life—Switzerland—Fiction.   3. Orphans—Fiction.
4. Switzerland—Fiction.]   I. Krupinski, Loretta, ill.   II. Title.
PZ7.S772Ham   1996   95-21079
[Fic]—dc20   CIP
                                                                                                 AC

Typography by Christine Kettner
1   2   3   4   5   6   7   8   9   10
❖
First Edition

To Katherine, my editor and kindred spirit,
with gratitude and appreciation

The wind whistling through the fir trees woke me from my first night's sleep in the Swiss Alps.

I had met my grandfather for the first time the day before. My aunt Dete had brought me here to live with him on his mountain. I had lived with my aunt since my mother and father died when I was a baby. But now she had been offered a job in Frankfurt and could no longer take care of me. Grandfather was not pleased, and argued loudly with Aunt Dete.

After she left, Grandfather and I ate homemade bread and cheese with the best milk I'd ever had—fresh goats' milk. Later we made a bed for me out of hay up in the loft. The sweet scent of hay filled my dreams.

The next morning, I looked out my "Window to the Stars," as I had already named it. Grandfather was talking to a young goatherd. His name was Peter, and he soon became my best friend. They were surrounded by goats from the village. Schwänli and Bärli, Grandfather's goats, were there too.

When I came down from my loft, I could see that

Grandfather had been very busy. He had made a chair just the right size for me. I knew then that I would be staying to live with him.

I climbed up to the pasture with Peter and the goats. All I could hear was the whistling of the wind and the tinkling of the goats' bells. The wildflowers made a colorful quilt beneath us.

By the time the changing season brought a colder wind, Grandfather and I had grown to love each other very much. We were a family. He taught me how to make cheese from Schwänli and Bärli's milk.

Winter changed our life in the mountains. Peter and I could no longer go up to the pasture with the goats. He lived farther down our mountain in a poor hut with his mother and his blind grandmother, whom he called "Oma."

When the weather allowed, Grandfather would wrap me up like a present and we would sled down the mountain to visit Oma.

I wished I knew how to read, since Oma had lost her sight and loved books so. Instead, we told each other stories while she spun yarn, needing only the touch of her fingers to guide the wool.

The seasons passed around, and around again. Spring arrived like a lost friend. Aunt Dete arrived too. She told Grandfather that she wanted to take me back to Frankfurt with her. I'd never seen Grandfather so angry.

Aunt Dete said she knew a wealthy family in Frankfurt looking for a companion for their frail daughter, Klara. Klara needed a wheelchair to get about. My aunt said that I could learn to read and write there.

But Grandfather did not want me to leave, and I did not want to go. She packed the few things I had anyway and hurried me away with the promise I could soon return. I cried all the way down the mountain.

In Frankfurt, I lived with the Sesemann family in a grand house that was bigger than any in the village back home. I was a companion to Klara, who was a few years older than I, and we instantly took a liking to each other. A tutor  came daily, and a kindly doctor came often to visit Klara. The doctor and I became fast friends.

Because her mother had died and her papa was often away on business, we were cared for by the housekeeper, Fräulein Rottenmeier. She presided over the household like a queen. Cheerless, she gave orders and found fault with everyone, especially me.

I often told Klara about my life on the mountain. She said, "I would love to see your mountains, but I don't think the doctor will ever let me make the trip."

I, too, began to fear that I would never see my mountains again.

Soon after I arrived, I grew homesick. All I had seen in Frankfurt were streets and buildings—I missed the fir trees and flowers. One day I spotted a church with a tall steeple. I climbed the stairs to the top, hoping I would see my mountains. Instead, rooftops and chimneys reached as far as I could see.

I was very sad until the church's caretaker showed me a basket of kittens. I knew Klara would love them, so I took some kittens back with me. Fräulein Rottenmeier had quite a different opinion. She sent the kittens right back.

She told me later I was naughty and ungrateful.

Klara's father, Herr Sesemann, was a kind man and treated me as if *I* were his daughter too. His visits were never long enough.

Herr Sesemann often planned surprises for us. One time it was a visit from Klara's grandmamma.

And so it was that another kind-hearted grandmother came into my life. Although the tutor had tried to teach me to read, it was Grandmamma who succeeded. She gave me a beautiful book of stories and pictures, which I read to her and Klara.

Still, I was homesick. Soon I grew thin and pale, and every night I dreamed of my life on the mountain.

They told me later that I was sleepwalking. While I was dreaming of running in the pasture, I would walk out of the house in my nightgown. For a while everyone thought the house was haunted, but the ghost turned out to be me.

My sleepwalking made the good doctor realize how frail my health had become. He advised Herr Sesemann to send me home immediately.

When I returned to my mountains, Grandfather could not believe his eyes. When he hugged me, he said he could feel my bare bones. Peter made me promise never to leave the mountains again, and with all my heart I promised.

First I danced among the fir trees and listened to them whispering with the wind. Then I climbed up to my sleeping loft to look out my Window to the Stars. I was home again. Grandfather gave me two bowls of sweet goats' milk instead of one.

When we visited Peter's hut, I took the big book that Grandmamma had given me. I placed it in Oma's hands and said, "I have a surprise for you. I have learned to read." We spent the winter reading together.

Months later, a letter from Klara arrived, and I read it to Grandfather. She wrote, "Our good friend the doctor is coming to visit you to see if I might make the journey this summer."

When the doctor arrived, he brought us lovely gifts from the Sesemanns. He quickly understood why I love my mountains so. He learned that the mountains could heal body and soul. Before he left, he told me that he thought a visit would be good for Klara.

Grandfather and I were ready when Klara and Grandmamma finally arrived. He had made extra stools for everyone. I had set out jugs of wildflowers and a jar of fresh honey, ready to be spread on homemade bread, in our outdoor dining room.

When Klara arrived, she told me that my mountains were even more beautiful than I'd said.

Grandmamma told Grandfather, "Many a king would envy this tiny empire."

I pushed Klara everywhere I could in her wheel-chair. I introduced her to Schwänli and Bärli. Together, we listened to the wind whistling through the fir trees favoring us with their piney scent.

Grandmamma was going to spend the evening in the village and visit another day. Before she left for the night, I heard Grandfather tell her that he thought a few weeks instead of just a few days of mountain air and sweet goats' milk might give Klara new strength. Grandmamma heartily agreed.

Klara and I could scarcely believe our ears, for we had never expected to be together again for such a long time.

Klara could barely sleep on her first evening in the hayloft. She lay looking out my Window to the Stars. Back in Frankfurt, the curtains were drawn before the stars came out. We spent the days telling each other stories and giggling about Fräulein Rottenmeier.

Klara wanted to see the pasture and spend more time with Peter, but it was too difficult to push a wheelchair there.

Grandfather often urged Klara to try standing. Standing was painful for her at first, but the sunshine and sweet goats' milk were giving her new energy. We all hoped that Klara might learn to walk again. Every day Grandfather helped her practice standing.

One day, Grandfather carried Klara up to the pasture. He said he would be back later to carry her down the mountain.

After lunch, Klara was eager to see the place where my favorite patch of wildflowers grew. She looked so forlorn, and it was such a short walk away, that I asked Peter to help. Klara stood and leaned heavily on both of us.

Klara took one small but firm step. She clenched her teeth from the pain, but she kept trying. Peter and I cheered her on. Klara took another tiny step, and then another, and cried out, "Heidi! Peter! Look at me! I won't need a wheelchair ever again."

With Klara still leaning on both of us, we walked farther up the pasture. There we rested on a blanket of wildflowers. It was a happy day for us all.

When Grandfather came to fetch us, we surprised him with Klara's good news.

"I knew you could do it!" he said. "We'll practice all week and then surprise your grandmamma."

When Grandmamma came for her visit, she was amazed to see Klara stand and take a few steps. Then in the midst of all our excitement, Klara stood up and looked down the path.

Grandmamma gasped—Herr Sesemann was waving his arms and climbing toward us. Klara leaned on me as we walked slowly down to greet him. A look of confusion on his face, Herr Sesemann stopped when he saw us coming down the path.

"Papa, don't you know me any longer?" shouted Klara.

Her papa hugged her tightly. I was the only one to see the tears of joy in his eyes.

Many more good things happened after that day.

On our way down the mountain, we stopped to visit Peter and Oma. Oma and Grandmamma had become friends during that summer and were sad to part. When she got home, Grandmamma made sure that warm clothes and a comfortable bed for Oma were delivered to the hut. And now every winter I go to school, because Grandfather and I live in the village when the snows come. I'm trying to teach Peter to read.

Best of all, Klara comes back every summer to visit. We race each other up to the pasture and sleep in the loft, where we look out my Window to the Stars and pretend we're in a carriage riding through the sky.

$\mathcal{A}$s a child, Loretta Krupinski lived in an urban area on Long Island, New York, a world far different from Heidi's alpine meadows, log huts, and majestic mountains. Ms. Krupinski's imagination was fueled by Joanna Spyri's vivid story. She longed to live high up in the Swiss Alps as Heidi did.

Now, many years later, it has been her pleasure to adapt the three-hundred-page classic novel for a younger audience. Heidi's story and her magical alpine world have been brought to life in glowing paintings just right for picture book readers.

$14.95

DATE			